Danger in Ancient Rome

RANGER in TIME

Danger in Ancient Rome

KATE MESSNER

illustrated by
KELLEY McMORRIS

Scholastic Press / New York

Library of Congress Cataloging-in-Publication Data
Messner, Kate, author.
Danger in ancient Rome / by Kate Messner ; illustrations by Kelley McMorris. —
First edition.
pages cm. — (Ranger in time)
Summary: The mysterious box that Ranger the golden retriever found in the
garden transports him back to first century Rome, where he must rescue
Marcus, a young servant boy, and Quintus, a volunteer gladiator, from the
brutal world of the Colosseum.
1. Golden retriever — Juvenile fiction. 2. Colosseum (Rome, Italy) — Juvenile
fiction. 3. Time travel — Juvenile fiction. 4. Gladiators — Rome — Juvenile
fiction. 5. Adventure stories. 6. Rome — History — Domitian, 81-96 — Juvenile
fiction. [1. Golden retriever — Fiction. 2. Dogs — Fiction. 3. Colosseum (Rome,
Italy) — Fiction. 4. Time travel — Fiction. 5. Gladiators — Fiction. 6. Adventure
and adventurers — Fiction. 7. Rome — History — Domitian, 81-96 — Fiction.]
I. McMorris, Kelley, illustrator. II. Title.
PZ10.3.M5635Dan 2015
813.6 — dc23 2014029202

ISBN 978-0-545-63918-7

10 9 8 7 6 5 4 3 2 1   15 16 17 18 19

Printed in the United States of America   113
First edition, July 2015

Book design by Ellen Duda

For Dominic,
who is always up for an adventure

Chapter 1

GLADIATOR SCHOOL

Marcus held his sword high in the hot Roman sun. Sweat dripped into his eyes, but he did not look away from his opponent. That was the first rule of being a gladiator. Defeat in battle always begins with the eyes, the writer Tacitus said.

Marcus crouched low. He shifted his weight from foot to foot. The other gladiator would be fast and strong. He would have to be faster and stronger.

Marcus leaped forward and jabbed with his sword.

Smack!

It hit the wooden post with a hollow thunk.

"Marcus Cassius!" Villius, the manager of the Ludus Magnus gladiator school shouted across the training ground. "Do you not have work?"

Marcus nodded and dropped the small wooden sword to his side. It was the only gift Villius had ever given him, a toy presented to him when he first came to live at the gladiator school five years ago, after his parents died in one of Rome's many fires. Marcus had been sold to Villius as a slave to pay off his father's debt.

Marcus had loved that toy sword at first. He'd played with it every day in the shadows as he watched the real gladiators train. But now that Marcus was eleven, the toy sword felt silly. He longed for the day he could use a real sword.

One day, Marcus would be a gladiator. One day, he would earn more than just his food and a corner in which to sleep. One day, he would win enough to have a real home of his own.

But today was not that day.

"We have a new man arriving this morning. Make a place for him to stay," Villius said. "The barracks are full, so he will share your cell. I will prepare his things for training." Villius stomped off toward the building where weapons were stored.

Marcus hurried across the arena toward the row of barracks. The sun had barely risen, but the day was already hot and muggy. The sharp smell of smoke filled the air.

Fires were common in Rome's crowded neighborhoods. Another blaze had ripped through the city last night. Another row of Rome's stacked-up apartments had burned to ashes while the emperor's fire brigade passed buckets from hand to hand, trying to put out the flames.

Marcus hated the smell of smoke. It reminded him of the fire that had taken his family and his home away.

He lived at Ludus Magnus now. Villius had told him he had a new family — *familia gladiatoria*. But this was nothing like home.

It had been five years of cleaning barracks, delivering messages, and swinging his wooden sword in the shadows. Sometimes, Marcus felt like it would never end. He was eleven now, and it would be five *more* years before he could become a gladiator himself. Then he would be the bravest in the arena. He would win fight after fight, the way Villius had won. That was how Villius had earned his position as head of the gladiator school. That was how Marcus would win his freedom.

But not today.

Marcus stepped into a tiny brick-and-stone room and spread out a bed of straw for the new gladiator who would arrive that morning. He was a volunteer — a free man who would take the gladiator's oath, hoping for victory and riches. When he signed the agreement, the new man would give away his freedom, promising to train and fight for a number of years. Marcus wondered why the man had decided to bind himself to the gladiator school. Some volunteers did so hoping to buy freedom for a friend or family member who was enslaved. Others longed for excitement and honor. They thought they would find those things in the arena.

Marcus recognized the hope in their eyes when they arrived. He understood that kind of hope. Five more years . . .

"Hurry up, boy, or there will be no bread for you!" Villius called from the center court.

Marcus finished with the straw and headed back to the training area.

Outside the walls of Ludus Magnus, the streets of Rome buzzed with morning work. Horses pulled carts. Food vendors called out for business. Inside, the sounds of gladiators in training filled the yard. Hector and Crixus grunted as they lifted weights. Apollo and Cleto sparred with heavy wooden practice swords on a platform until Apollo lost his balance and fell into the prickly straw below.

Cleto let out a growling laugh. He was the strongest of the gladiators here now, a fierce man with a thick scar across his chest. Cleto's muscles looked as if they were carved out of stone, and he had the temper of an angry bear. Marcus did his best not to cross Cleto's path if he could help it.

Another man, Typhon, clashed his wooden sword against the *palus*, the thick wooden post in the center of the training ground where Marcus liked to practice, too.

Whack! Whack!

Thunk! Whack! Crack!

Marcus watched Typhon, memorizing his moves, until Villius called to him. "Marcus Cassius! Come see to our new gladiator."

Marcus hurried to the gate to meet the new recruit, a young man named Quintus Flavius, who stood beside Villius. The new gladiator was tall with broad, muscular shoulders. He walked with a brave swagger but had a boy's round, pudgy face. His big eyes didn't have the hardness of the other fighters, but he was new. It would come. Until then, he would need to stay out of Cleto's way.

"Take Quintus to the amphitheater so that he might see some of today's games," Villius told Marcus. He turned to the new gladiator. "Then you will return to your cell. You are free to go to the baths or elsewhere in the city in the daytime. At night, you will be locked in. You belong to the *familia gladiatoria* now."

Quintus nodded, but Marcus saw a flash of uncertainty in his eyes. Maybe it was regret that he had signed over his life for the coming years. Maybe it was fear. Perhaps it was both.

"Come," Marcus said. "I will show you the amphitheater. The games will begin soon."

Chapter 2

SHOOT! SCORE!

"Come on, Luke! Go for it!" Coach shouted.

Luke dribbled the soccer ball between two defenders and gave it a hard kick, right into the goal.

Score!

Everyone in the bleachers clapped and cheered. Ranger barked. Sometimes the noisy crowd made him nervous, but this noise seemed to make Luke happy. That made Ranger happy, too.

"Good job!" Sadie gave Luke a high five after the whistle blew to end the game.

"That was some goal!" Dad said.

Ranger jumped up and licked Luke on the chin.

"Down, boy!" Luke laughed. "But thanks for the congratulations, if that's what you mean."

"I think that's exactly what he means," Mom said as she hurried Sadie past the playground at the edge of the soccer field. "We can come back to the park later. Dad's going to make us some brunch."

When they got home, Luke ran to set up the soccer net. "Want to play in the yard until it's time to eat, Sadie? I'll teach you how to head the ball."

"Okay!" Sadie ran to the garage to get a ball and tossed it out into the grass. Ranger started to chase it, but then . . .

Squirrel!

The squirrel raced across the yard, waving

its fluffy tail. Ranger had to leave the ball alone to chase it up a tree.

Luke laughed. "You can't be a soccer star if you keep chasing squirrels, Ranger." He jogged over and scratched Ranger behind the ear.

Ranger leaned his head into Luke's hand. Next to snuggling with Luke and Sadie, chasing squirrels was Ranger's favorite thing in the world. That was the only reason Ranger wasn't an official search-and-rescue dog. He'd gone through all the training with Luke and Dad. He'd learned to find missing people, even if they were in the water or in a building with lots of smoke. But to be a search-and-rescue dog, you had to ignore everything except your job when it was time to work. And Ranger couldn't turn down a good squirrel chase, no matter how much he wanted to please Luke.

"Ready, Sadie?" Luke called. He kicked the ball high in the air. Sadie raced to get under it, but she missed, and the ball bounced away. Sadie chased it, and Ranger was about to run after her when he heard a high-pitched humming coming from inside the house.

Ranger scratched at the door until Dad opened it. Then he went straight to the mudroom. There, the humming sound was louder. Ranger pawed through the blanket in his dog bed until he found the old metal first aid kit he'd dug up in Mom's garden. It had only made this humming sound once before . . . when someone really, truly needed help.

That someone was a boy named Sam who had been making a long, dangerous trip with his family and needed Ranger's help. Ranger had found Sam's baby sister when she ran off. He'd kept Sam from stepping on a rattlesnake, warned the family of a buffalo stampede, and rescued Sam's pa from a raging river. When Sam got very sick, Ranger had stayed by his side until he was better. Sam had understood, somehow, that Ranger couldn't stay with his family once their journey was over, and he'd given Ranger a quilt square when they said good-bye.

Now that bit of fabric rested next to the old metal box. And the box was humming again.

Ranger nuzzled the leather strap until the first aid kit hung around his neck.

The humming grew louder. Bright light spilled from the cracks in the old metal box.

It felt warm at Ranger's throat. The light beamed brighter and brighter, until it seemed to swallow up the whole mudroom.

Ranger's skin prickled under his fur. He felt as if he were being squeezed through a hole in the sky. All he could see was that bright, hot light. *Too bright!* He closed his eyes until the humming stopped and the hot metal cooled.

When he opened them, he found himself in a huge open space. This arena wasn't Luke's soccer place. Luke's soccer place smelled like grass and boys and hot dogs from the food truck at the edge of the field.

This place was much, much bigger. Many more people filled the stands. The seats were made of stone. The air was thick with heat and shouts and strange animal smells. The floor was covered in something gritty. Ranger lifted a paw and sniffed at it.

Sand.

Sweat.

And blood.

Chapter 3

A PARADE FOR THE EMPEROR

"Get out of there, dog!" Marcus darted out of the tunnel onto the arena floor. He grabbed Ranger by his leather collar and pulled him back into the shadows.

"Where did you come from? You sure are strange looking." Marcus knelt down to get a closer look. This fluffy, golden-colored dog looked nothing like the hounds that normally lurked around the arena.

Marcus lifted the old metal box from around the dog's neck, opened it, and peered inside. "Did Villius send you with these bandages and things? We don't need them now." Marcus tucked the metal box into a dark corner where two stone walls came together.

Ranger looked at his box. It had stopped humming. He looked down the tunnel into the dark. He looked out at the big stone arena.

Then Ranger looked up at the strange boy who had pulled him into the passageway. He was a little taller than Luke and stronger looking. He smelled of smoke and oil. His hands were rough. He stood beside a bigger boy, almost a man. That one reached down to pet Ranger. Ranger leaned into his hand and breathed in his scent. It was better than the sweat-and-blood smell of the sand outside.

The last time Ranger had found himself in a strange place with strange smells, it was because a little girl was lost. Ranger had found her and helped her family through a long, dangerous trip. But these boys didn't seem to be looking for anyone. What was Ranger supposed to do?

"Step back to make room for the men, Quintus. They are beginning the *pompa* to mark the opening of today's games," Marcus said. He, Quintus, and Ranger stood close to the stone wall. A band began playing — a fanfare of trumpets and horns and flutes — and two by two, the gladiators came walking past them in the tunnel. When the men stepped into the arena, the crowd exploded in cheers. Marcus couldn't wait until it was his turn to wear the fancy armor and carry a real sword.

"Will they all fight at once?" Quintus asked.

"No. This is a parade to honor the emperor before the program begins. The fighting will happen later this afternoon, after the wild animal fights and executions."

If the men parading past were scared, they were good at hiding it. They walked with their

chins high and their shoulders back, fearless. It would be a good day in the arena. "The crowd will like these matches," Marcus said as the men swaggered past. Slaves followed, carrying the gladiators' weapons.

The hair on Ranger's neck prickled. The air smelled of metal and sweat. And the sounds! *Clangs! Shouts! Cheers!* It was louder than a thunderstorm. At home, those always made Ranger hide under Luke's bed.

The crowd cheered so loudly, Marcus could feel it in his chest. Many shouted the names of their favorite fighters.

"Felix!"

"Beryllus!"

"Soon, Quintus, they will be shouting your name," Marcus said, "and one day, they will shout my name, too."

The arena had filled quickly. The common

men and women sat up high on the third tier. Senators sat closer to the action, and Rome's leader had the best view of all.

"Is that Emperor Domitian?" Quintus asked, pointing to a tall balding man with big eyes. He stood at his seat right in front, at the center of the arena.

"It is indeed," Marcus said. He hoped Domitian would still be emperor when he became a gladiator. Domitian was not easy to please. He had a reputation for being cruel. Some people even said he had killed the former emperor, Titus, his own brother. But Domitian loved the games. Marcus knew that when his time came, he would fight bravely and make his emperor proud.

When the last gladiator strutted out onto the arena floor, Marcus looked behind him. "We should leave the tunnel now. The wild animal hunt will begin soon," he said. He pointed deeper into the shadows, where slaves were pulling on ropes and moving machinery. "Let's go below."

"Very well." Quintus waited for Marcus to lead him down the hallway.

Marcus hesitated and looked down. He was still holding the dog's collar. The dog looked up at him and tipped its head as if to say, "Where next?"

What was Marcus supposed to do with this stray? Villius wouldn't be pleased if he brought it back to the gladiator school. He couldn't let it run loose into the arena. It would be killed when the animals were released. So Marcus kept hold of Ranger's collar and headed down the tunnel.

It was dark at first, but soon, torches on the walls lit the way. Ranger didn't like all of the open flames. The flickering light and shadows made the hair on his neck prickle.

Marcus walked them down a damp stone staircase that led to another level, below the arena floor. "Stay close to me, dog. You do not want to meet the animals down here."

Ranger sniffed the musty air.

Stone and dirt.

Metal and rope.

Men and sweat and . . .

Cat?

Ranger stopped so quickly that Marcus tugged his collar. Quintus continued on down the hall.

"Come on, dog. This way."

Ranger stayed put. He lowered his head and sniffed at the bottom of a metal cage. It was too dark to see inside. But Ranger didn't need to see. He could smell.

Cat!

Ranger sniffed again. This wasn't the cat-smell of Ruggles, the black-and-white cat who lived with the family next door to Luke and Sadie. This was *different* cat.

Big cat!

"Boy, get back to work!" A burly man in a brown tunic hurried up to Marcus and lifted a long stick with a hook at the end. Marcus jumped and let go of Ranger's collar. Ranger backed away from the man with the stick but stayed close to Marcus.

"I work for Villius at Ludus Magnus," Marcus explained. He looked around for Quintus, but the gladiator-in-training was gone. "I was told to —"

"We must prepare the animals for the hunt. Can you handle a lion?" The man gestured toward the cage. A lion stood inside, cramped and restless.

Marcus swallowed hard. He wanted to run, but he took a deep breath. Gladiators did not run from lions. "Yes. Of course I can."

"Then open the cage so that I can lead this beast to the lift."

Marcus reached for the rope that held the cage door closed. His hands trembled. He stepped back. "I am sorry. My master told me to —"

"You are here now, and you shall work for me," the man growled.

Ranger growled, too. The man laughed and pushed him aside with his stick.

Ranger growled again, but he stayed back. Ranger knew from the dog park that big, growling dogs could be trouble. This hulking man looked just as dangerous. Marcus needed help. He needed the bigger boy to return.

The man with the stick shoved Marcus toward the cage. "Lift the latch and step out of the way!" he ordered.

Ranger looked down the hallway. The stone passageway was shadowy and confusing.

The air was damp and full of smells. But among the sand and strange men and big cats, the smoke and dust and people-sweat, Ranger picked out a scent he recognized — the boy-man with the warm, rough hand. Ranger could find him!

Ranger was good at finding. In search-and-rescue training, Ranger had found Luke hiding inside a hollow tree in the woods. He'd found Sadie hiding in a barrel on a practice course. Ranger could find anyone, anywhere. When he did, Luke always gave him a drink of water and hugs. And then they went home.

Home.

Ranger would find Quintus and bring him back to help Marcus. Maybe then, his job would be done and he could go home.

Chapter 4

FINDING QUINTUS

Ranger wanted to run, but he had to be careful. He couldn't lose Quintus's scent. He padded down one of the shadowy passages, sniffing the dusty stone. Quintus had come this way for sure.

Ranger kept his nose to the ground, where the scent was easiest to find. There were so many other smells filling the air.

Animal smells. Big cats — lots of them — and other animals that Ranger didn't recognize.

Smoke from a faraway fire.

And men. So many men.

They were everywhere in these underground passageways. They were muscular and sweating, carrying supplies and working machinery. But none of them were Quintus. Where was he?

Ranger could still smell his scent trailing through the air. But before he followed it much farther, Ranger had to go to the bathroom. He usually liked to go on a tree, but this didn't seem like the kind of place trees would grow. Maybe he'd find a gate that led outside.

Ranger followed the gladiator's scent to another passageway. Here, filthy men in tunics were tying ropes. Others were holding wooden bars that stuck out from a post that went from the floor to the ceiling. Beside them was a wooden platform with trees growing on it.

Trees!

Ranger started toward them and picked out a tree. It didn't smell quite right. It didn't look right, either. Most trees grew out of dirt and not wood, but a strange tree was better than no tree at all. He trotted up to it and lifted a hind leg.

Before he could finish, one of the men shouted and grabbed for Ranger's collar. Ranger tugged away from him. Then, the men holding the wooden bars started pushing them around in a circle. The center post turned. Ropes wound around it, and Ranger felt the platform rising under his paws. He was being lifted, along with the not-quite-right trees, toward a hole in the ceiling.

One of the men called out an order. The others pushed harder on their wooden bars. The lifting machine creaked, and Ranger rose higher above the stone floor, closer to the ceiling. The roar of people echoed down through the hole. The lifting machine was raising the trees up to that other level of the amphitheater.

Ranger did not want to go back to the

blood-smelling sand. He did not want to go back to the noisy crowd. He had to find Quintus so he could go home!

The rope men grunted and tugged. Ranger was being lifted higher and higher above the stone floor. He would have to jump.

Ranger found a space between two men and leaped from the platform. He heard another shout. Someone grabbed at his tail as he ran. When Ranger was away from the men and the lifting machine, he sat down and licked his paw. He'd scratched it on the hard stone floor when he landed. It was tender, but he was not hurt badly.

Ranger put his paw down and lowered his nose to the ground.

The Quintus smell was gone.

Ranger stepped out from the shadows and sniffed some more.

Nothing.

He did not want to go near the trees and the lifting machine again, but that was where the smell was. Carefully, Ranger padded back toward the men and the ropes. He walked slowly, sniffing at the gritty stone floor.

Finally . . . *there!*

Ranger followed the Quintus smell up one passageway and down another. The smell grew stronger until finally, Ranger trotted up to Quintus himself. The young gladiator was crouched in a dark corner, staring out at the activity.

Ranger ran up to him and nuzzled his hand.

"You found me, dog," Quintus said, reaching up to scratch behind Ranger's ear.

Scratches were nice, but not now. There was no time. Quintus had to come back with Ranger to help Marcus.

Ranger nudged Quintus's shoulder and barked.

"What is it?" Quintus said.

Ranger barked again. He took two steps back toward the passageway that led to the animal cages and Marcus. He whined and waited for Quintus to get up and come with him.

But Quintus shook his head. "I'm not going back. I . . . I never should have come here."

Ranger didn't understand what Quintus was saying. He only understood that Quintus was not moving. And that was a problem.

Ranger barked again and jumped up on Quintus so suddenly, he almost pushed him right over. He barked and nudged and whined and nuzzled.

"All right then, dog!" Finally, Quintus stood up and followed Ranger down the passageway.

Whenever Quintus stopped, Ranger ran around behind him and nudged him to keep going. They walked around a corner, through one stone doorway and then another. They were getting closer to Marcus. Ranger could smell him. But Marcus wasn't alone.

There were more big cats in the cages that lined the passages, Ranger could tell. He could hear their throaty growls. He could smell their meaty breath. It made Ranger's fur prickle, but he couldn't turn back.

Ranger kept going, even when men started opening cages. They prodded the animals out into the passageway and coaxed them onto the lifting machines. Ranger kept his eyes straight ahead, searching.

He didn't see Marcus.

But he heard him scream.

Chapter 5

LION ON THE LOOSE

"Help! Please . . ." Marcus felt the big cat's claws poking through the thin material of his tunic. It had happened so fast! At first, when he'd lifted the latch to let the lion out of its cage, the creature cowered in a corner. But then the trainer had prodded it with his sharp stick, poking and teasing, urging it to move.

That's when the lion bounded from its cage. The animal trainer jumped out of the way, but Marcus wasn't ready. The lion knocked him to the stone floor. He hit his head on the edge of a stair. When the walls stopped spinning, there was the lion. It pinned Marcus down with a fat, heavy paw. Marcus whimpered. He didn't dare move.

The animal trainer scrambled to his feet, picked up his pointed stick, and crept toward the lion. The beast gave a deep, growling roar. The vibrations echoed in Marcus's chest. He stared at the animal's gaping mouth, its sharp, yellowing teeth, its hungry pink tongue.

"Help . . . please . . ." Marcus whispered. But the animal trainer took a step back.

The lion's fierce golden face was so close, Marcus could feel its steaming breath on his cheek.

Then Marcus caught a flash of movement in the passageway. "Quintus!" he whispered. Quintus was a gladiator — a new one, for certain — but he was brave and strong. Quintus would save him! "Quintus," Marcus whispered

again. He was scared to make noise, lest the lion stop growling and start tearing him apart.

"Be still," Quintus said. "Be still . . . and . . . and then . . ." Quintus didn't finish his thought. Marcus heard the fear in his voice.

Ranger heard it, too. He didn't understand this place of fighting and moving trees and strange animals. But he understood fear. Marcus was in trouble.

Ranger took a step closer to the lion and barked. He growled deep in his throat and pulled his lips back to show the big cat his teeth. At home, that made Ruggles the neighbor cat run under the porch.

But this was not home. There was no porch. Only a dead-end passageway with hard stone walls.

And this cat was not afraid.

The lion turned its enormous head and looked at Ranger with big yellow eyes. It kept Marcus pinned to the damp stone floor. Marcus struggled to breathe. The lion's sharp smell stung his nose. Tears spilled from the corners of his eyes. Why had he said he could handle a lion? How had he imagined controlling this creature so many times his size? He was weak and foolish and probably about to be eaten.

The lion's tail twitched.

Ranger barked again. He looked up at Quintus, then took a careful step toward Marcus and the big cat.

The lion lifted its paw from Marcus, turned, and opened its mouth in a roar that seemed to shake the whole amphitheater.

Ranger held his tail high and stiff. His fur prickled all along his spine. He leaned forward to make himself look as big as he could and started barking, again and again.

The huge cat launched itself at him.

Ranger leaped out of the way. He landed hard on the stone floor and crouched low, growling. The lion lowered its body, too. Its muscles rippled under its matted fur.

Marcus rolled away from the big cat and struggled to stand up. His chest ached. His legs trembled underneath him. His knees were almost too weak for him to stand, but Quintus reached out a strong hand and pulled him to his feet. Marcus stumbled to the stone wall. Beside him, the animal trainer raised his sharp stick and took a quiet step toward the lion.

Its body was all muscle, low to the ground. Ready to explode.

Ranger was ready, too. He locked his eyes on the big cat's snarling face. Every hair on his body stood up.

The lion let out another thunderous roar and sprang.

Ranger jumped to the side just as the animal trainer jabbed the lion with his stick. The huge cat roared and reared to face him.

Then four more men came running with sticks and swords and nets. They snared the big cat and tied it tight with thick ropes. It was over in an instant, and the men led the lion off to one of the lifting machines.

Marcus looked up at Quintus. His voice shook. "Thank you."

"I do not deserve your thanks." Quintus looked at the ground. "I did nothing. I was afraid."

"But you came back," Marcus said.

"The dog brought me." Quintus knelt, and Ranger walked up to them. He let Quintus scratch behind his ear. Then he turned and nuzzled Marcus's hand until the boy began petting his head. It helped Ranger's fur settle down again.

Marcus squatted, face-to-face with Ranger. "Thank you, dog. You are the bravest of us all."

Ranger didn't understand the boy's words, but he recognized the tone of his voice. It was the same tone Luke used when Ranger had done his work in search-and-rescue training. Ranger would find the person he was supposed to find in the woods or the training course, and Luke would say, "Good job, Ranger! Good job, boy!"

He would give Ranger hugs and a drink of water, and they would go home.

Home.

Ranger looked down the long stone hallway toward the lifting machine. A lion's roar echoed off the stone. Ranger smelled animal droppings, metal, and fear.

Marcus gave Ranger another pat on the head and sighed. "Perhaps I am not ready to be a gladiator."

"I fear I will never be ready," Quintus said quietly.

"You will," Marcus told him, standing up. "We must go back to the barracks now. Villius will be waiting. You will train, and you will be ready." He paused. "You will have to be."

Chapter 6

FIGHTING LESSONS

When Marcus and Quintus walked through the tunnel that led from the amphitheater back to the gladiator school, Ranger followed them.

Villius met them at the gate. "Why have you been away for so long?" He cuffed Marcus on the shoulder with a rough hand. Before Marcus could answer, Villius's eyes fell on Ranger. "And what is this hairy monstrosity?"

"Just a dog. He's a stray," Marcus began. Even though there were plenty of cats around the gladiator school, he should have known that Villius would object to such a big, strange-looking dog. Marcus thought about putting the dog out into the streets, but he couldn't bring himself to leave it. Not after what had happened. "He got into the amphitheater somehow, and . . ." He trailed off and glanced quickly at Quintus, silently begging him not to speak of the lion. Villius would be furious if he knew Marcus had abandoned his own duties to work for the animal trainer.

Quintus seemed to understand. "The dog has taken a liking to us, it seems," Quintus said, reaching down to pat Ranger's head.

Villius grunted. "He will be taking a liking to *your* share of meals if he stays. I have no food for the beast." He gave Quintus a wooden training sword and gestured to the open space at the center of the school. "Now get to your training. Cleto will practice with you today."

Marcus looked out at the oval ring. Cleto stood with a wooden sword in his hand and a snarl on his face. "He is brutal. But if you move quickly, you will be a match for him," he told Quintus. "He is strong but slow. When you —"

"Are you a trainer now?" Villius interrupted, mocking him. Marcus lowered his head. "Take the dog and go empty the pots."

"Come, dog," Marcus said quietly, and slapped his knee.

Ranger followed him to a very small room with stone walls and a mound of straw in a corner on the floor. Marcus flopped down in the scratchy stuff and started talking, even though there were no people around to answer. Luke did that in his bedroom sometimes, too, especially when he was upset.

"He thinks that I am nothing, dog. But I *could* be a trainer," Marcus said. Ranger pawed at the straw and sat down beside him. Marcus scratched behind his ear and sighed. "I have watched the men come and go for five years. I know what it takes to be the best. I could win in the arena. I know I could!" He picked a small stick out of the straw and stood up, holding it as if it were a sword.

"A hit up here" — Marcus whacked at the top edge of the barracks door with his stick — "is a blow to the head. Swing lower, and you have hit your opponent in the flanks. Strike here, and you take his knees out from under him." Marcus swung the stick at the lower edge of the door. The stick broke in half, and he was left with a tiny stub of make-believe sword. The other half went flying into the straw.

Ranger bounded after it. He loved to play fetch! Ranger nuzzled the straw aside until he found the stick, took it in his teeth, and trotted over to Marcus by the door.

The boy smiled and accepted the other half of his sword. "I thank you. But I fear this weapon cannot be repaired." He tossed it to the ground. Ranger pounced on it and brought it back again, wagging his tail. Marcus laughed. He threw the broken stick-sword. This time, Ranger jumped up and caught it in midair.

Again and again, Marcus threw and Ranger fetched. It felt good to jump and play, even in the small cell. For a few minutes, Ranger could almost imagine he was home in the yard, playing fetch with Luke and Sadie, or chasing after soccer balls at the park.

But then the door flew open.

Marcus dropped the stick and rushed to lift the pot from the corner of the cell as Villius shoved Quintus into the tiny room. "A poor effort," he declared. "Lock him in for the afternoon. He has not earned his time in the city.

Bring him a bit of barley gruel for supper, and we shall try again tomorrow." He stomped off.

Quintus sank into the bed of straw and buried his face in his hands. Ranger sat beside him. Sometimes, when Luke was upset, that helped. But it didn't seem to be helping Quintus.

"I never should have sworn the gladiator's oath," he said. "I will not survive my first fight in the arena."

"You will," Marcus said. He dug through the straw until he found both halves of the stick-sword. He kept one and handed one to Quintus. "Take this. Stand up, and I will show you."

Ranger thought they might both throw sticks for him now — Luke and Sadie did that sometimes — but instead, Marcus stood with his stick-sword held firmly in one hand. The other hand, he held to the side, balancing himself.

"The trick is to strike and move before your opponent can strike back," he told Quintus. He poked with his stick and darted to one side before Quintus could react. "Now you try."

Quintus swung at Marcus with his stick-sword. Marcus saw it coming and easily lunged out of the way.

"You are too slow that way," Marcus told Quintus. "You must stab with the tip instead of slashing with the side." He demonstrated. Quintus tried again and managed a good stick-sword poke at Marcus's shoulder.

"Very good!" Marcus said. "When you train, you will learn a series of moves like this. Take care not to follow the practice too closely when you go out to fight in front of the emperor. The audience loves a good show. People hate a fight played too close to the book."

Quintus took a few more jabs at Marcus before his stub of a sword flew from his hand. He let out a breath and sank down in the straw to pat Ranger's head. He looked at the door to the barracks and then at Marcus. "I think I will go to the baths before the evening meal," he said.

"Not today," Marcus said. "Villius has ordered you locked in your cell."

"Surely, he would not want his new recruit to become ill?" Quintus stood and started for the door.

"You must not. If Villius finds that you have disobeyed, he will be furious." Marcus peered out at the yard. Apollo was fighting Cleto in practice. Villius shouted for them to stand taller, hit harder.

"He will not know that I am gone if you do not tell him," Quintus said. "I am simply in need of a bath so that I might feel like myself again. Would you deny me that after I kept your secret from the amphitheater?" He raised his eyebrows and looked at Marcus.

Marcus swallowed hard. It would be a while before the barley gruel was prepared. He nodded quickly. "Go. Be quick." Quintus slipped out the door, and Marcus lowered himself to the straw. He stroked the soft fur behind the dog's ears and yawned.

Marcus's legs still felt weak from what happened at the amphitheater. Now that the lion was locked up again, now that he was safe, he was so very, very tired.

Ranger stretched out in a small patch of sun. Marcus lay down beside him and closed his eyes.

When he woke up, Villius was shouting in his face.

"Where is he? What have you done?"

Marcus scrambled to his feet and looked around. The sun was low in the sky. He must have slept for some time. Quintus should have come back long ago, but he was nowhere to be found. "I . . . I do not know. He asked only to go to the baths, and —"

"You disobeyed me?" Villius pinned Marcus against the stone wall of the barracks. His snarl was every bit as fierce as the lion's.

Ranger's muscles tensed. He growled low in his throat, but he didn't move. He sensed that anything that made Villius more upset would also make him more dangerous.

"You will go. You will find him." Villius's breath was hot and sour on Marcus's face. "And you will bring him back. Or you will pay with your life."

Chapter 7

THE RUNAWAY

Villius stormed out of the barracks, and Marcus sank to his knees. He would never find Quintus. Quintus had lied to Marcus about going to the baths. He had hated this place and fled. Now Marcus was left to pay the price. He buried his face in his hands.

Ranger brought him a stick.

Marcus didn't look up. Ranger nudged him until he moved his hands and saw the gift. Marcus took the stick for a second, then dropped it back in the straw.

Ranger picked it up again. He wasn't sure

what else to do. How could he make things better for Marcus?

Ranger gave Marcus another nudge with the stick, but this time, Marcus ignored him. So Ranger kept the stick in his mouth. It was Quintus's stick-sword. It smelled like Quintus. Maybe Quintus could help. Ranger had found the older boy once; he could find him again.

Ranger dropped the stick and sniffed the air. He walked to the door and sniffed again. Quintus's smell was there, with the smoke and barley soup and straw.

Ranger barked.

Marcus looked up.

Ranger barked again. He ran back to the stick and picked it up, then ran to the door and pawed at the ground.

"You are right, dog. I must go." Marcus stood up and started for the door. He paused to pick up his small wooden sword from the floor and sighed. "I will never find him, but I must go and try."

Ranger sniffed the air and started toward the gate to the school. Quintus had gone this way. His scent was still strong in the air.

Marcus followed the dog into the streets, where food vendors were calling out.

"Honey cakes!"

"Sausages!"

The games at the amphitheater had ended for the day. Crowds of Romans spilled out the gates into the street.

There were so many more smells now.

Horses!

Dust!

Sausage!

But Ranger stayed focused on the Quintus smell. When he lost it for a moment in the crowd, he circled back until he found it again.

There! Ranger followed the scent away from the school and the arena, toward another big building made of stone.

"The baths?" Marcus said. Had Quintus told him the truth after all? Marcus was afraid to hope, but the dog was insistent as it led him past a juggler near the entrance, toward the courtyard of the Baths of Titus.

A man stopped Marcus. "Where is your ticket?"

"I am not here to bathe," Marcus told him. "My master has sent me to find someone."

The man let him pass, and Marcus followed Ranger into a larger open space. It was full of sweating, groaning men lifting lead weights and exercising before they went for their baths. Servants waited with flasks of oil. The hair-plucker squawked, calling for customers. But Quintus was not there.

Ranger could still smell him, though. Quintus had been here, even if he wasn't anymore. Ranger lifted his nose and led Marcus into a room where men were soaking in a pool. One plunged in and splashed Ranger's legs with cool water. Ranger kept going, through a doorway into another room with another pool and then a third water place where the air was hot and steamy. Here, too, the bath was full of men, but none of them were Quintus.

Ranger led Marcus back out to the street. The smoke smell was getting stronger, but Ranger could still pick up Quintus's scent. He held his nose high and kept going.

Marcus followed Ranger. They jumped from stone to stone across the road and dodged a cart barreling toward the Forum. When they turned a corner, a broken pot came flying out of an apartment window and smashed to the stones right in front of them.

Ranger jumped back, then stepped carefully among the shattered pieces. His paws were already sore and raw from walking so far.

"Where are we going, dog?" Marcus hesitated. "The Forum? Quintus would not have come here, to the city center with all of its courts and busy markets. Not if his hope is to escape."

Ranger paused, too. He took a few steps back and made a circle. Quintus had come this way, he was sure. But the scent was getting weaker. He nudged Marcus in his hindquarters to get him moving again.

They hurried along the stone road, past olive and fig trees. They ran past the Temple of Jupiter with its tall, brightly colored columns. Marcus searched the faces in the crowds they passed. None of them belonged to Quintus.

Marcus was hungry and exhausted. Soon, it would be dark. He was out of hope and out of time. His only chance was to go back to the gladiator barracks and beg for Villius's mercy. Marcus was about to turn around when a man ran past him in the Forum. Many more followed, all shouting the same thing.

"Fire!"

Chapter 8

RESCUE FROM THE FLAMES

Marcus raced after the crowd with Ranger on his heels. When he turned a corner, his breath caught in his throat. The fire from last night was back. It had swallowed up a row of shops and the apartments above them. Women in the street screamed out for family members still inside. The slaves in the fire brigade passed buckets from hand to hand. But the fire was too big, too hot. It crackled and hissed as it devoured the wooden buildings.

The air was thick with black smoke. It

stung Ranger's eyes and nose. But he caught a familiar scent floating by with the ashes.

Quintus!

Ranger turned in a careful circle. There it was! The Quintus smell! He nudged Marcus and started to track the scent closer to the burning building, but Marcus didn't follow. Ranger jumped up on him and pushed his paws against the boy's chest.

Marcus pushed him back with his wooden sword. "No, dog! We can go no closer. It is too dangerous." The fire had spread to the bakery next door.

Ranger jumped again and barked. Marcus turned, just as Quintus came running through the crowd.

"Help!" He grabbed Marcus by the shoulders and turned to look at the bakery and the apartment above it. "My brother!"

Marcus sucked in his breath. The air was steaming hot, but he shivered. "He is inside? Is that your family's home?"

Quintus choked out his answer. "Yes!" He held his head in his hands for a moment. Then he took off toward the burning building.

Marcus sprinted after Quintus, coughing and gagging on the thick smoke. Ranger followed. He stayed as low to the ground as he could. The air was so dark and thick, it was hard to see anything. But he could smell Quintus, even through the smoke.

They had just reached the building's front door when someone shouted, "Watch out!" A roof beam came crashing down to the street and exploded in a shower of sparks and ash.

Marcus looked up at the flames pouring from the building now. If Quintus's brother was inside, he did not have much time to get out. "Where is he?"

"He should have been preparing the ovens. Gaius! Gaius!" Quintus shouted into the flames. For a moment, the fire seemed to pull back. Quintus stepped inside the doorway. "Gaius!" He bent to pick something up, then called for his brother again.

But the wind blew hard, and the flames rushed up in a roar. Quintus stumbled back outside, overcome by the heat. He looked down at his hands and shook his head. "He did not answer. But his *tali* were on the floor." Quintus opened his hand to show a set of dice made of bone.

Ranger stretched up to sniff them.

"No, dog!" Quintus pulled back his hand. But Ranger had smelled something. Bones. And a person smell, too. Maybe the Gaius person Quintus was calling.

Ranger had practiced finding a person in a burnt-out building with Luke and Dad once.

But that fire had already been put out. This one was hot and live and spreading.

Ranger stepped up to the door of the building and barked. The person smell from the dice was strong here. The person had to be close, but Ranger couldn't see him. Not with the hot wind and smoke swirling all around. He waited until the wind died down for a moment and the fire shrank back, deeper into the building.

It was still hot — *so hot!* — but Ranger crept low to the floor. There! There by the long stone counter, a boy sprawled on the floor. Ranger barked at him.

Danger!

Get up! Come!

The boy rolled to his side, but he did not get up.

Ranger ran to the boy and barked again. The air was too hot, too smoky. The boy had to leave. He had to get out with Ranger. But no matter how many times Ranger nudged the boy's chest with his nose or licked his face, the boy did not open his eyes.

So Ranger did what he had learned to do when he found a person in the woods. He stayed. And he barked.

The fire was spreading. *Too bright! Too hot!* It would be in the kitchen soon.

Ranger tried to bark louder, but the smoke made his mouth dry and rough. He never had to bark this long practicing with Dad and Luke. When Ranger found the person and barked, Luke came.

But he wasn't coming this time. Ranger barked until his whole throat burned. Finally, Quintus and Marcus crashed through the door, coughing and waving their arms in front of them.

"Gaius!" Quintus cried, and raced to his brother's side. He lifted the boy by his arms and dragged him toward the door.

Marcus dropped his wooden sword on the floor and grabbed Ranger's collar. "Come on, dog! We have to get out!"

The summer wind blew hard, fanning the flames. Pieces of ceiling fell in burning scraps around them. Marcus couldn't see anymore. He couldn't hear Quintus over the roar of the flames. He could only feel the dog under his hand, leading him.

Finally, they burst out onto the street. Marcus stumbled across the stones, away from the rushing flames and the thick smoke. He sank to the ground with Ranger beside him.

Quintus dragged his brother over. The boy was awake now, coughing and gagging.

Marcus looked up at Quintus, then back

at the burning building. The top floors were starting to cave in. "Where is the rest of your family? Are they —"

"No," Quintus said. "It is only Gaius. My mother is dead, and my father left long ago to work in the quarry. Gaius is all that I have." Quintus let out a sharp breath. "He could have died."

"We *all* could have died." Marcus glared at Quintus. "Where did you go? You told me you were going to the baths. You told me —"

"I know." Quintus sank to the ground. "I was going to run. I went to the baths first, but then got to thinking." He shook his head. "I am no gladiator. Cleto knows it. Everyone knows. So I was going to run. Disappear." He looked up at the burning building as another beam crashed to the street. "I came to say good-bye to Gaius, but now —"

Villius's sharp, deep voice cut him off. "Now you will come with us!"

Marcus looked up. Villius and Cleto stood above them in the street. Both held their swords, ready to strike. Cleto twisted his mouth in a sneer.

Marcus stepped back. He looked at Ranger, then up at Villius. "Please . . . we found him. As you ordered."

"You did indeed," Villius said. His eyes blazed with anger. He held a thick length of chain in one hand. "And we will be certain he does not leave again."

"But my brother . . ." Quintus began.

"We will care for him until you are free," said a woman who lived nearby. She knelt beside Gaius and looked up at Quintus. "You must do as he says."

Quintus blinked hard and turned to go

with Villius and Cleto. Marcus and Ranger followed them through the smoky night. They marched past the torch-lit amphitheater and back to the gladiator barracks. Villius shackled Quintus with a thick iron cuff around his ankle and locked him into the barracks, along with Marcus and Ranger.

Quintus collapsed on the straw. He was asleep before Marcus could think of anything to say.

Marcus sank down on his own pallet, and Ranger settled next to him.

"Thank you, dog," Marcus whispered. "If you had not found him, it would have been worse."

Ranger nuzzled Marcus's hand, and the boy stroked his head. The pets got slower and slower until Ranger knew Marcus was asleep. Then he waited for something to happen.

He'd done his job. Hadn't he?

Ranger waited for the "Good boy! Good job!" He waited to hear Luke's voice. He waited for his cool drink of water, but his throat stayed dry and smoky.

How many times would he have to find Quintus before he could go home?

Chapter 9

SWORDS, SHIELDS, AND ARMOR

Marcus woke to Villius's barking voice. "Marcus Cassius! Get yourself up and bring Quintus for training!" Villius threw open the barracks door and tossed Marcus a bit of bread and cheese.

Marcus rose from his straw pallet and belted his tunic. He gave Ranger some water and a crust of bread, then nibbled the rest as he shook Quintus awake.

"Do you have water?" Quintus asked, grimacing. His voice was sandy and hoarse. "And food?" His eyes fell on the bread and cheese in Marcus's hands.

"Here." Marcus handed Quintus his flask for a drink. He broke off some cheese and bread to share, even though he knew there might be no more food until dinner. Villius would not be generous, with the mood he was in today.

"I am grateful," Quintus said, taking a swig of the water. He bit into the crusty bread and looked around. "Villius brought us nothing more to eat?"

"To punish you for running, and me, for failing to keep you here," Marcus said. "But do not worry. You will have dinner tonight. It is not in Villius's interest to let you starve. The crowd loves a strong gladiator."

Quintus scoffed. "The crowd must love Cleto."

"They do." Marcus nodded. "He fights bravely. He must. He has a wife and child at home. He will do anything to win his freedom so that he may return to them."

Quintus's face fell. Marcus wished he could take back the words. He knew what it felt like to have no one. "And you have your brother."

"That is why I must win my freedom. To protect him." He stretched his arms above his head. They were scratched and bruised from the rubble of the fire.

Marcus's memories of family had faded. He never cried for his parents anymore. But Marcus wished he had a brother to protect him. He felt a hot sting in his eyes, and a tear slipped down his cheek. He turned away so Quintus would not notice.

But Ranger saw. It reminded him of the time Luke had been hurt at a soccer game and had to be carried off the field. Ranger had run right up to nuzzle Luke's face. He had seen this same look in Luke's wet eyes — a mix of hurt and brave. Ranger stepped up and tried to nuzzle Marcus, too, but the boy pushed his nose away.

Marcus blinked hard and turned to Quintus. "If you are to win your freedom, you will need to train hard. You must learn to use the weapons better than anyone else."

"Villius will never teach me now." Quintus dropped his arms to his sides. "He is furious. He wants only to see me lose."

"Then I will teach you myself," Marcus said. He thought Quintus might laugh and was glad when he did not. "I have been here for five years. I have seen all of the best gladiators train. Tigris and Beryllus and Diomedes and Cleto, too. I have watched them fight and learned their moves." He looked at Quintus. "I will teach you everything."

Before Quintus could answer, Villius burst into the cell. He removed the shackle from Quintus's leg. His ankle was swollen and raw.

"Take him to be outfitted," Villius told Marcus and stalked out into the courtyard.

"This way," Marcus told Quintus, and led him across to a large stone building with a guard posted outside.

"Our new gladiator needs weapons and armor," Marcus told the man.

The guard looked Quintus up and down. "Villius says he is to be a *retiarius*." He disappeared into the storage room.

Marcus's heart sank. His expression must have shown it because Quintus looked alarmed. "What is it? Is that not a good thing?"

"No, all is well," Marcus told him. "You will have a bit of armor, plus a trident and net to trap your opponent." Quintus looked relieved to hear that. Marcus did not want him to know the truth, that the *retiarius* was the lowest of all the gladiators, that he almost always fought a heavily armed *secutor* in the arena. And worst of all, that Cleto was a *secutor*.

The weapons guard returned with a trident — a long stick with a sharp, forked end — a net, and a protective guard to fit over the shoulder. "This goes on your left arm," the man told Quintus. Then he brought out a large wooden sword and shield. "These are only for training."

Ranger sniffed at the pile of weapons. He smelled wood and metal. Men and their sweat.

Quintus reached down to pick up the shield. "So heavy!" he exclaimed. Then he lifted the sword. "And this as well."

"That is to prepare you," Marcus told him. "Set the net and trident aside. For now, you will practice with the wooden sword and shield. They are twice the weight so that your real weapons feel light and handle easily on the day of the games. Now come with me. Villius will be waiting. It is time for your training to begin."

Chapter 10

PREPARING TO FIGHT

All morning long, Quintus practiced at the *palus*. For now, he did not use the net and trident. He worked only with his heavy wooden shield and sword to build his strength.

Ranger found a nearby patch of shadow and sprawled in the dirt. His ears pricked up every time Cleto came near, but the older gladiator ignored Quintus and kept to his own training.

Marcus brought Ranger a bowl with some water and set to his work. He cleaned out the barracks. He delivered messages for Villius. He emptied the pots in the cells and collected the urine to use for washing clothes later. When he could, he came back to the center of the training yard to watch and call out advice.

"When you strike the *palus*, you must think of it as your opponent," he told Quintus. "Remember that a high strike —"

"Is a blow to the head. I know! But I have no more hits in me. I can barely lift my weapon anymore." Quintus dropped his sword and shield to the ground and bent over to catch his breath.

"Keep practicing," Marcus told him. "You will get stronger."

There was no break for food at midday, but Villius gave Marcus a few coins and sent him to one of the street vendors outside the Ludus Magnus. He brought Quintus bread and a small bowl of stew with *garum*, a sauce made of fish, salt, and spices, left to rot in the sun.

Ranger sniffed at the bowl. It smelled rancid and sharp, like garbage left out too long in summer.

But Quintus practically inhaled the meal. He saved the last of his bread for Ranger.

"I wish I had more than a bit of crust to thank you with, dog." Quintus stroked the fur on Ranger's back as Ranger scarfed down the bread. "You saved my brother's life."

Quintus turned to Marcus. "And I must also thank you," he said. "I do not know why you are so kind to me. I will repay you when I can."

"You will need to train harder to do that." Marcus handed him a flask of water. "Now back to the *palus*. Imagine that you are in battle with Cleto. You must win to survive."

Quintus spent the rest of the afternoon training with the wooden sword, whacking the *palus* as if it were his opponent. He practiced high blows to the brute's head and low hits to his legs. Quintus held his heavy shield steady and maneuvered to be ready, just in case the wooden post ever struck back.

Once, Villius stopped to watch him. Marcus thought he saw a flash of admiration in the manager's eyes. But it was only there for a moment before he turned and walked away.

That night, there was barley gruel for dinner, for Marcus and Quintus, too.

Marcus left a bit of his in the bowl. "You must be hungry, too, dog." He set it down, and Ranger trotted over to lick it out.

"He can have some of mine as well," Quintus said, and started to lower his bowl.

But Marcus said, "No. You must eat all that is offered to you. You must grow stronger. It is your only chance."

Quintus nodded slowly and lifted the bowl back to his mouth. Ranger was only a little

sad about that. The gruel was like gritty, salty oatmeal. Ranger licked out Sadie's oatmeal bowl after breakfast sometimes, even though he didn't like oatmeal much. Luke's bacon was so much better.

Ranger missed bacon. He missed Sadie and Luke and the house and the yard. He even missed oatmeal. What was he supposed to do in this strange, sweaty place?

He'd been waiting for people to rescue. He'd been watching for ways to help. But all Quintus did was bang that stick against the wooden post. All Marcus did was watch Quintus and tell him how to hit the post better, harder, more. All Villius did was shout at Marcus. All Cleto did was scowl and glare.

And all Ranger wanted was to go home.

• • •

Days passed. Ranger wasn't sure how many. Every one started the same way — with a hunk of stale bread and a wedge of old cheese. Then Quintus and the other gladiators went back to the post-whacking and sword-lifting. Sometimes, Quintus used his new weapons — the trident and net — and trained with an older gladiator whose arms and chest bulged with muscles. Quintus's arms grew bigger, too.

Every night, Ranger curled up beside Marcus and nuzzled his hand. But a straw pallet was not a bed. And Marcus was not Luke.

Finally, one morning, trumpets blared in the distance. Villius appeared as the sun was rising. "It is time," he told Marcus. "The emperor has called for three days of games. Prepare Quintus. This time, he shall fight."

Marcus jumped from his straw pallet. "But he has not had enough training. He is not —"

"He is ready. And he owes a debt for his escape." Villius narrowed his eyes and looked straight at Marcus. "On the day you failed to keep watch as you were ordered."

Marcus swallowed hard and lowered his eyes. He knew that Villius could have had him beaten or even killed for failing to do his job. But he had escaped punishment . . . so far. "I will prepare Quintus as you ask," he told Villius. Then he looked up. "With whom will he be paired in the arena?" he asked, even though he could have guessed the old gladiator's answer.

"Cleto," Villius said, a smile creeping over his face. "I am sure they will put on a most excellent fight for the emperor."

Chapter 11

LET THE GAMES BEGIN

"When will I learn the name of my opponent?" Quintus had been pressing Marcus for answers all morning. "Will it be a gladiator from another school?"

"I am not certain," Marcus lied. He was afraid that telling Quintus about Cleto would fill him with too much fear to even enter the arena. "Just remember," Marcus told Quintus as he helped him into his armor. "You must trap him with the net. It is the only way to be victorious."

"I do not believe there is a way at all,"

Quintus said, strapping on his shoulder plate. "But I will fight as I have been taught." He took a deep breath and paused to look at Marcus. "As *you* have taught me. Thank you, my friend."

"Brother," Marcus said quietly. "We are brothers in the *familia gladiatoria*."

Quintus nodded and picked up his net. Marcus lifted Quintus's trident. He pointed it toward the tunnel that led from the gladiator school to the center of the amphitheater. "Let us go. The *pompa* will begin soon."

Ranger followed them into the tunnel. He kept a distance from Quintus as they walked through the flickering torchlight. Ranger knew all of the gladiators from the training yard, but he hardly recognized them in their armor and helmets.

It reminded Ranger of the autumn night at home when Luke's and Sadie's friends came to the door with masks and strange clothing. Ranger could smell their regular scents. He knew they were only children — just Alex and Tyrell and Zeeshan and Noreen. But their costumes still made the hair on his neck stand up.

Quintus made Ranger nervous today, too, with his armor-plated shoulder and net. Ranger pricked up his ears and held his tail straight.

When they reached the amphitheater, men were lining up to go through the gate for the parade.

Quintus tipped his head toward the first group of men. They were tied together with ropes and wearing nothing but rags. "Why do they have placards around their necks?" he asked Marcus.

"To announce their crimes. These men will be executed at midday," Marcus answered, and bent to pet Ranger. He always tried not to look at the criminals in the parade. It made it harder hearing their cries later on.

"Look who approaches," Quintus said, and drew in a breath. Marcus stood and saw Cleto strutting down the long stone hall. He carried his metal helmet under his arm. Quintus started to look down, but Marcus nudged him.

"You must not look away from your opponent," Marcus hissed.

Quintus's mouth dropped open. "My opponent? Cleto is my opponent? If I am to fight Cleto with nothing but a shoulder guard for armor, then I might just as well . . ." His voice trailed off. He looked at Marcus. "You knew."

"Forgive me," Marcus pleaded.

Quintus glared at him. "You knew and did not tell me."

"There is no time for this now. You must meet his eyes," Marcus whispered, nudging Quintus to turn and face Cleto as he passed. "Defeat in battle always begins with the eyes. That is what Tacitus said. Meet your opponent's eyes to tell him that you are not afraid."

"That would be a lie," Quintus said quietly. But he lifted his chin and looked directly at Cleto. "Today, we will learn who is the stronger man."

Cleto let out a growling laugh and glared at Quintus.

Ranger understood that kind of look from the dog park. If you looked away, you were the weaker dog. Quintus could not afford to be weak. Ranger moved quietly to Quintus's side and leaned his body against him.

Quintus met the older gladiator's gaze without blinking. Finally, Cleto turned away and strutted off to find his place in the parade.

"You will walk beside him," Marcus told Quintus, putting a hand on his elbow to guide him into place.

Quintus jerked away from him. "I will find my own way."

Through the gate, Marcus could see the arena floor and the mobs of Romans filling the seats of the amphitheater. When the music started, Marcus took a deep breath and looked up at Quintus. "I know that you are angry. I did what I thought was best. I remain your brother." He put his hand on Quintus's back and gave a gentle push. "I will be right behind you with your trident."

Horns played, and the music carried them out onto the sand-covered floor of the arena. Ranger stayed back in the tunnel; he hated the sand under his paws. And the noise! The mob was many, many times bigger than the crowd of families and friends who came to eat hot dogs at Luke's soccer games. Ranger sniffed the air.

People! So many people!

There was food — sausage and cakes and the rotten fishy smell.

There were animals — big cats and more. Too many for Ranger to think about.

He could sense the people's excitement, too. It was different from the energy in the air at Luke's soccer games. Wilder. More dangerous.

Ranger stood in the shadows and watched until Quintus and Marcus finished their march around the arena and stepped back into the tunnel.

"You are ready, my brother," Marcus told Quintus.

Quintus looked at Marcus, and his face softened. "I will never be ready for this. But thank you for standing with me."

Marcus nodded. "They will call for you when it is time."

"Move out of the way!" shouted the animal trainer, pushing Marcus to one side. He rushed through the tunnel along with a group of *bestiarii*, the men trained to hunt wild animals as a show for the crowds.

Marcus leaned out from the shadows to watch through the open gate.

As the *bestiarii* rushed into the arena, scenery began to rise from the floor.

"It is as if the trees grow by magic!" Quintus said, staring.

"They are brought up from below through the trapdoors," Marcus explained. "So are the animals for the hunt."

Marcus couldn't control the pounding of his heart when the first lion appeared. Was it the same big cat that had pressed its paw to his chest and breathed its hot, meaty breath on him? He swallowed hard and kept talking, hoping his words might hide his fear. "Now here come more lions. . . . Now an ostrich . . . and leopards . . ."

"May the gods have mercy," Quintus whispered. His eyes were wide.

"Perhaps we should step away," Marcus said, urging Quintus deeper into the tunnel. Seeing the blood and battle would not be good for his brave spirit. To fight Cleto, Quintus would need all the courage he could find.

"Quintus, have I told you about the gladiator Proximus who was here some time ago? He knocked Villius from the platform in training one day . . ." Marcus told stories to distract Quintus from the screams and cheers that echoed down the stone tunnel from the arena. Ranger sat beside them until the animal hunt and executions ended and the first round of gladiators had finished their battles.

Then Villius appeared, with Cleto sneering beside him. He looked as if he had already won the fight. And Villius looked hungry to see Quintus fail.

Marcus had seen that look before, when it had already been decided that a fight would end only with a gladiator's death. Often, a gladiator losing a fight could submit by lifting a finger to end the match. Then the crowd could ask the emperor to show him mercy. But the look on Villius's face told Marcus that would not happen today. Quintus would have to do more than fight bravely. He would have to win. If he submitted, even if the crowd wished to spare his life, it might not happen.

Marcus looked up at Quintus and whispered, "You must not submit. No matter what."

Quintus's eyes clouded over. "I cannot beat Cleto. Surely, if I fight bravely —"

"No! Listen to me. Do. Not. Submit. If you do, they will not spare you. Not after what has happened."

Quintus's eyes grew wider. Marcus handed him his net and trident. He adjusted the bronze plate over Quintus's shoulder, his only protection. It was nothing compared to the long shield Cleto would carry. "Are you ready?"

Before Quintus could answer, Villius took him roughly by the arm. "It does not matter if a gladiator is ready. He fights when it is time." Villius shoved Quintus down the tunnel and through the gate, out onto the arena floor.

The crowd went wild.

Chapter 12

BLOOD IN THE SAND

Out in the arena, Cleto raised his hands above his head. He turned so the crowd could see his muscles.

Quintus stood staring, his shoulders hunched.

"Quintus!" Marcus screamed from the tunnel entrance. Somehow, Quintus heard him over the roaring mob and turned to look. Marcus motioned for him to turn and show himself off like Cleto. Quintus did, and the crowd cheered even more loudly.

The arena officials spoke to the people while the gladiators prepared to fight.

Cleto lowered his helmet over his head. It covered his entire face. Marcus couldn't even see his eyes through the dark holes in the metal mask. Cleto wore a loincloth, leg plates, and metal armor over one arm. He carried a long shield and a sword that gleamed in the sun.

Beside him, Quintus looked practically naked. A *retiarius* wore no helmet and no leg armor — only a bit of protective strapping wrapped around one arm, a bronze plate on his shoulder, and a loincloth around his waist. Quintus's only weapons were the net and trident. He'd barely had time to practice with either.

Now it was too late for training.

The arena official gave the signal to begin the match. The crowd's roar grew louder.

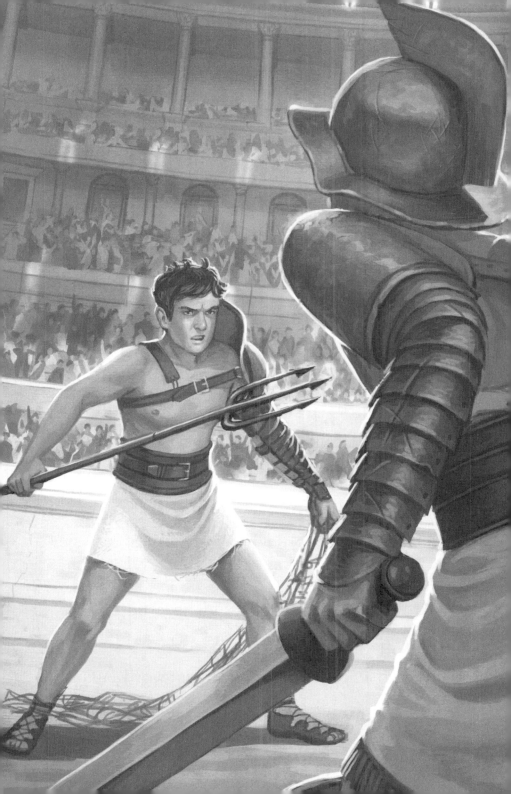

Ranger whimpered. Marcus lowered a hand to stroke the dog's head but kept his eyes on the arena.

Right away, Cleto lashed out with his sword and jabbed at Quintus's unprotected shoulder. Quintus dodged the blow and whirled to face Cleto. He thrust his trident forward. It clanged against the older man's sword.

The crowd cheered, but Marcus cringed. Had Quintus learned nothing in training? *Your net!* Marcus wanted to scream at Quintus. *Use your net!* But Quintus would never hear him over the crowd now.

His trident would be worthless unless he could snare Cleto. Without the net to slow Cleto down, Quintus would have no chance at all.

Cleto leaped forward with his sword. Again, Quintus jumped out of the way. He finally threw his net while Cleto was regaining his balance, and the lead weights at the edge of the net carried it toward its target.

Yes! Marcus thought. It was good aim. But the net slipped over Cleto's helmet onto the sandy floor. Quintus lunged to pick it up, and while he was bent down, Cleto slashed with his sword.

Quintus fell back, clutching his upper arm. Even from the faraway tunnel entrance, Marcus could see blood seeping from between his fingers.

But Quintus didn't rest for long. He had his net back. When Cleto came at him again, he threw it with all his might. This time, Quintus held on to the end of the net. The rest of it snagged Cleto's sword and tangled around his legs. Cleto stumbled and flailed, trying to free himself, as Quintus approached with his trident.

Marcus held his breath. Quintus might actually win. *Do it!* Marcus thought. *Careful . . . Wait . . . Now!*

But Quintus hesitated. And in that moment, Cleto cut through the net with his sword. He slashed at Quintus's arm again, and this time, a bigger gash opened, spilling blood into the sand.

Quintus dropped his trident and grabbed at his wound, then fell to the ground.

The crowd roared. Cleto played to them. He untangled himself from the net and pumped his fist in the air. He picked up Quintus's trident from the sand and flung it to the side. Then he raised his sword and looked down at his opponent.

Marcus squeezed his eyes closed and sank to the stone floor. He couldn't watch it happen. He couldn't stand to watch his only friend, his *brother*, die in this fight. He pressed his fists hard into his eyes, felt the dog leaning against him, and tried to disappear. But he couldn't escape from the sounds. The screaming and clapping and stomping of the frenzied crowd. He waited for the scream, the final roar.

Instead, he heard a sharp bark.

And Ranger took off running.

Chapter 13

DOG IN THE ARENA

Ranger burst into the hot sun of the arena floor. He ignored the gritty sand that irritated his paws. He ignored the too-loud screams of the crowd. He ignored everything except the two men at the center of the amphitheater and raced toward them, barking as loud as he could.

The crowd's shouts turned to a gasp — one great, collective breath of surprise. What was a dog doing in the arena during the fight?

Ranger kept barking.

Cleto turned in surprise, his sword still poised to strike. But before he could act,

Ranger leaped at him. He tackled Cleto, the way he tackled Luke when they were rough-housing in the yard at home.

Cleto tumbled backward. He didn't laugh like Luke would have. Even through the dark holes of the metal mask, Ranger could sense the anger in his eyes.

Cleto sprang to his feet and whipped around.

Ranger bounded away. He raced around the arena, running in a circle close to the crowd. They were cheering now, cheering for him, as if he were part of the show, brought in by the emperor to entertain them like the ostriches and lions and gladiators.

Marcus heard the cheers and opened his eyes. He couldn't believe what he was seeing. The dog had stopped the fight!

Cleto stood at the center of the arena, turning in confused circles as Ranger galloped around him. Quintus struggled to his feet, blood dripping from his wounded arm. He limped toward his net, all wadded up on the sandy floor.

He needs more time, Marcus thought. He clutched his hands together and prayed to the gods for help. Maybe if the dog kept running, kept playing the clown . . .

But in that moment, Cleto remembered his opponent. He was not entertained by Ranger's antics like the crowd was. Just as Quintus was reaching for his net, Cleto jumped in front of him and lifted his sword.

"No!" Marcus sprung to his feet and raced from the tunnel. He screamed until his lungs burned. He waved his arms wildly, the way the trainers did to distract a runaway animal so it could be snared.

Cleto only lifted his gaze for an instant. But that was enough.

Ranger bounded across the sandy floor, barking and barking. Cleto spun around, and when he did, Quintus flung out his net with all his might. The leaden weights clinked against Cleto's shield as the net wrapped around him.

"Your trident!" Marcus pointed to where it lay in the sand. Quintus limped toward it as Cleto freed himself from the net. He struggled to untangle his sword and shield. When he realized they were hopelessly snared, he threw off his bulky helmet, rushed at Quintus, and slammed his body against him.

The two men tumbled through the sand, with flailing arms and pounding fists. Both were filthy and exhausted. Cleto was atop Quintus when the arena official's sword dropped between them.

"Enough!"

The two men froze mid-battle. They stared at each other, out of breath. Their lips were curled, their eyes empty. Sweat poured down their temples.

Ranger stopped running. He stood next to Marcus, panting in the muggy afternoon air.

The arena official took hold of the two gladiators' wrists, one in each hand, and pulled them to their feet. Then he turned and looked up into the stands, to the balding man in the purple robes. Emperor Domitian had risen to stop the fight at the request of the screaming mob.

Marcus looked up, waiting for what he knew must come next. The emperor would raise one hand to declare either Cleto or Quintus the victor. Then the crowd would decide the fate of the other man. Marcus knew what would happen if Quintus lost.

Marcus thought he might suffocate on the muggy amphitheater dust. It felt as if the two men had used up all of the air in the arena during their fight. But Marcus made himself keep breathing, keep watching.

The emperor stared down at the gladiators. Marcus wished he could see inside the man's mind. Both men had fought bravely, but only one must be declared the winner. Would Quintus be killed because he had lost his weapons and suffered a wound?

Marcus held his breath.

Chapter 14

THE EMPEROR'S DECISION

The emperor didn't move.

Marcus tried to read the expression on his chiseled face, but it was impossible. Perhaps Domitian would spare Quintus, even if he lost. But deep down, Marcus knew that was too much to hope for from a ruler who was famous for his cruelty. Why would he show mercy to a gladiator who had broken all of the rules?

The arena official stood on the floor waiting, still clutching the two gladiators' wrists, looking up at Domitian. The arena fell silent. The emperor stared back.

Then the crowd began clapping again, slowly at first, then faster and faster until their hands and stomping feet made a thunder that seemed to shake the whole amphitheater.

Finally, the emperor raised both of his hands, and the mob let out a roar louder than any other.

Marcus gasped. The emperor had declared *both* men victorious!

The arena official lifted both of their hands high into the air. It seemed as if the screaming and chanting and stomping and clapping might never end.

When it finally did, the official wrapped a piece of cloth around Quintus's wounded arm. The emperor sent men down with gifts for both of the gladiators. There were palm leaves for victory and — wooden swords! Marcus felt his eyes fill with tears. Quintus had won not only his fight but his freedom! The rare gift of the wooden sword from the emperor meant that a gladiator's service was at an end.

Quintus was free!

And that meant Quintus would soon be gone.

Marcus turned away. He squatted down to pet the dog and tried to hide the tears welling up in his eyes. He knew he must be happy for his gladiator brother. Perhaps one day, he would fight as bravely. One day —

"Boy!" Marcus felt a rough hand around his arm. The official pulled him up and turned him to face the edge of the arena. "The emperor has called for you. And your dog as well."

Marcus swallowed hard. He was responsible for the dog that interrupted the fight. Surely, he would be punished for interfering with the match. He took a deep breath, looked down, and put a hand on Ranger's warm head.

Somehow, it made him feel less alone in the big arena.

When Marcus lifted his gaze, Domitian was staring down at him.

The emperor motioned to a servant on the arena floor, an older man who walked with a slow limp. The man stepped up to Marcus and Ranger. He knelt down slowly and ran a hand over Ranger's fur. When he stood, he gave Marcus a palm leaf. "Today's victory is yours as well," he said. Then he held out a wooden sword. It was so much larger and heavier than the toy Marcus had lost in the fire.

Marcus stared at it. Certainly, this could not have the same meaning as Quintus's sword. He reached out for it. "Thank you," he said, then paused. "Is it a toy?"

The servant tipped his head. His thin white hair fluttered in the hot breeze. "It is your freedom, young man. If you are wise, you will show your thanks to the emperor now."

Marcus turned and bowed deeply. The crowd's shouts roared in his ears.

When he stood again, he looked at the old man who had presented him with the sword. "I am most grateful. But I do not understand," he said. "I am no gladiator. I have not fought for the emperor or the people of Rome."

"No. You are right about that. You have not," the man said. His eyes looked tired, but they crinkled at the corners when he smiled. "But today, you and your dog gave them the one thing they love more than blood." The servant looked up at the crowd of Romans, still on their feet, still cheering. "You gave them a story. One they will tell for a long time to come."

Marcus looked up into the stands until the cheers faded and the people began filing out through the amphitheater's numbered doors to go home. When he turned back to the arena floor, Cleto was already walking out through Porta Triumphalis, the gate of the victors.

But Quintus stood waiting for Marcus. He gestured toward the same gate. "Shall we go? We are free now, my brother."

"We are." Marcus looked up at him. "You can take your winnings and go home now, to your real brother and the bakery."

"The trouble is, we are in need of more help." Quintus's face was smeared with sweat and drying blood, but his eyes lit up when he grinned. "And you must remember, I have two brothers now. Will you come work with us?"

Marcus clutched his wooden sword so hard the splinters pricked his palms, but he hardly felt them. "Yes! Of course I will. Thank you!"

"I am glad." Quintus looked down at

Ranger. "Perhaps we will have a bakery dog now as well."

Marcus knelt down and scratched Ranger behind his ear. Then he flung his arms around the dog's neck and whispered, "Thank you, dog."

Ranger leaned into the whisper and the snuggle, but another sound made his ears prick up.

A high-pitched humming.

Ranger stepped back from Marcus and tipped his head. The sound was coming from the tunnel that led into the arena. Ranger took a few steps that way. The humming grew louder.

"Where are you going, dog? You must come with us. The victors' gate is this way." Marcus pointed in the other direction, but Ranger didn't come. He took another step toward the tunnel.

"He will come if he wishes," Quintus said quietly. He put an arm around Marcus and looked thoughtfully at Ranger. "But perhaps this dog has another home."

Home.

Ranger was ready to go. But first, he trotted back to Marcus for one last scratch.

"Don't you want to come?" Marcus knelt down, scratching Ranger behind the ear. "We are free now. You will have a home with us at the bakery!"

Ranger looked back at the tunnel. The humming was growing louder.

Marcus sighed. "Whether you come with us or not, you must have this." He tore a blade from his palm leaf. "Today's victory was yours as well as ours." He swallowed hard and tucked the leaf under Ranger's collar. "I will never forget you, dog."

The leaf was scratchy, but Ranger didn't paw at it. He gave Marcus one last nuzzle, then turned and walked into the cool dark of the tunnel.

Ranger followed the humming sound to a corner of the stone walls. He found the old first aid kit, right where Marcus had tucked it on the day Ranger had arrived. When Ranger nuzzled the dusty strap over his head, the humming got louder. It drowned out the wild animal sounds coming from the amphitheater basement and the people noises of Rome spilling in from the street.

Ranger saw a pinprick of white light escape from the corner of the old metal box. It grew brighter and brighter until Ranger had to close his eyes.

He opened them just in time to see Sadie kick the soccer ball past Luke, into the net.

Chapter 15

HOME

"No fair!" Luke yelled, booting the ball back out into the lawn. "I wasn't ready." He looked down at Ranger. "Where'd you go, Ranger? Have you been running through Mom's garden again? What's that?"

Luke reached for the palm leaf and pulled it out from under Ranger's collar. "Where'd you get this?"

Sadie ran up to see. "It looks like a leaf from Nana's palm tree in Florida."

"We don't have palm trees here." Luke frowned. Ranger nudged Luke's hand with a wet nose. "Don't worry." Luke laughed and tucked the leaf back under Ranger's collar. "Wherever you found it, it's yours to keep, Ranger."

"Who's ready for pancakes and sausage?" Dad called from the front porch.

Sadie and Luke raced for the door. Ranger started to follow them, but he stopped at the bottom of the steps and breathed in all of the home smells.

Luke and Sadie.

Grass and soccer ball leather.

A faint whiff of Ruggles, the next-door cat.

And sausage! *Home* sausage!

"Come on, boy!" Luke held the door open, and Ranger bounded up the steps to follow him inside. Before Ranger went to the kitchen to lick the sausage grease off Mom's hand, he stopped in the mudroom.

Ranger wiggled the leather strap from around his neck, and the old first aid kit dropped onto his dog bed. It was quiet now. No more humming.

Ranger pawed at his collar until the palm leaf slipped out. It dropped to the pillow, next to the old quilt square Ranger had brought back from his last adventure.

He could still smell Marcus's scent on the leaf. Marcus had his family now, with Quintus, Ranger was certain. Marcus had a brother, and a home.

And now Ranger was home, too. He gave the palm leaf one last sniff and pawed at the wool blanket on his dog bed until the metal box, the quilt square, and the palm leaf were covered up. Then Ranger padded into the kitchen, licking his chops.

His job was done. It was time for sausage.

AUTHOR'S NOTE

How do we know what we know about ancient Rome when so little was written down? Many of the history keepers of this time were poets and artists. In their verses, sculptures, mosaics, frescoes, and even graffiti, they've left behind details that we can read to learn about this culture.

The mosaics in Rome's Galleria Borghese, for example, show several pairs of gladiators fighting. These mosaics were once the floors of Roman houses and are now not only works of art but an important piece of the historical record. They depict different types of gladiators, all with specific kinds of weapons and armor. The *retiarii*, like Quintus in this story, were gladiators who represented fishermen, with their nets and tridents. The *secutors*, like Cleto, were known for their swords, long shields, and the helmets that covered their faces.

Some popular books and movies portray gladiator contests as fights to the death every time, but history doesn't support that story. More often, historians now believe that when one gladiator was wounded badly or signaled defeat by raising a thumb or finger, the match would end. While some who lost were then killed at the urging of the crowd, most were spared. They'd be sent back to the gladiator school to see a doctor, then allowed to recover and train so that they could fight again. Gladiators were expensive to feed and train, and their managers preferred not to lose them.

When Quintus and Cleto fight each other

in this story, both are declared victors. That's an unusual ending for a gladiator fight, but there is evidence that it happened at least once in history. The poet Martial left behind a rare, detailed account of a match from the opening games of the Colosseum in 80 AD, in which two gladiators, Verus and Priscus, fought in a match that seemed as if it might go on forever. Martial wrote about the emperor's declaration of a dual victory in his work called *De Spectaculis* (*On the Spectacles*):

> An end, however, was found for the well-matched contest:
>
> Equal they fought, equal they resigned.
>
> Caesar sent wooden swords to each, to each the palms of victory.
>
> Such was the reward that courage and ability received.

In researching *Ranger in Time: Danger in Ancient Rome*, I read many of these historical accounts and also traveled to Italy to see what remains of the world that Marcus and Quintus inhabited. I visited Pompeii, an ancient city whose history was preserved when it was buried by the eruption of Mount Vesuvius in 79 AD.

Many buildings, sculptures, frescoes, and graffiti survived because the city was preserved under the pumice and ash of Mount Vesuvius for nearly 1,700 years before archaeologists uncovered it. Today, it's still possible to walk through Pompeii's amphitheater and gladiator barracks and to stand on the stepping stones that allowed ancient Romans to cross their busy, dirty streets.

My family and I walked along the storefronts and saw the counters where food vendors would have called out for people to buy sausages, cakes, and stew with the popular fermented fish sauce called *garum*.

I also spent several days doing research in Rome. While Rome is very much a modern community now, it also remains a city full of ruins.

I explored what's left of the Roman Forum and the Baths of Titus, where Marcus and Ranger searched for Quintus. Reading the ancient poet Seneca's description of public baths helped me to imagine the sights, smells, and sounds of the first century:

> *Consider all the hateful voices I hear! When the brawny men exercise with their lead weights, I hear their groans and gasps. Or when someone else comes in to get a vulgar massage: I hear the slap of a hand on his shoulders. Add those who leap into the pool with a huge splash. Beside these, who at least have normal voices, consider the hair plucker, always screeching for customers, and never quiet except when he's making someone else cry.*

Each day, walking from our apartment into Rome's city center, we passed the remains of the gladiator school Ludus Magnus, just up the street from the Colosseum.

I imagined what it would be like to be Quintus, stuck in one of those small cells

and preparing for his day at the arena. Half of the small training arena at Ludus Magnus has been excavated. The other half still sleeps under a city street, lined with shops and pizza places in the shadow of the Colosseum.

Standing in the Roman Colosseum itself — the Flavian Amphitheater, as it was known at the time — was an experience I will never forget. Some of the stone from the ancient amphitheater was hauled away to be used in newer buildings, including St. Peter's Basilica, as Rome moved away from its violent past. But enough remains that it was possible for me to look out over the floor of that great arena and imagine how the crowds might have sounded when Quintus and Cleto stepped out to fight.

You might notice that the empty arches in the next photograph are full of statues on the cover of this book. At the time of the

gladiator games, those arches were indeed filled with painted statues of emperors and gods. When we see this kind of ancient Roman sculpture in a museum today, it is almost always a striking, plain white. However, by using chemical analyses and ultraviolet light, archaeologists have recently discovered that those "classic white" sculptures in ancient Greece and Rome were actually painted in bright colors.

The lower level of the amphitheater has also changed a lot since the time period in which this story takes place. Still, the ruins provide an amazing window to the past. It is still possible to see parts of the elevators and other machinery that slaves used to raise scenery and wild animals up to the arena floor.

It was impossible for me to read about the gladiator fights, to stand at the center of that great amphitheater, without wondering how such a brutal sport was allowed to go on. At the time, the gladiator fights were part of a tradition in ancient Rome. Historians believe it probably began with sacrifices made at funeral ceremonies and evolved into the popular entertainment held in large arenas throughout the Roman Empire. The games were free to attend in Rome. Anyone could obtain a ticket and sit with his or her social group. The emperor and senators had the best seats, while the commoners and most women sat in the upper level.

Historians believe the gladiator fights may have been a way for the emperor to keep control of his citizens. Life wasn't easy for the masses in ancient Rome. There were food shortages. The crowded wooden apartment buildings caught fire easily and burned quickly. One of those fires, in 64 AD, burned for six days, then rekindled for another three and destroyed more than half of the city. The Roman poet Juvenal used the phrase "bread and circuses" to describe the emperors' distribution of food and the spectacles of the chariot races and gladiator games for entertainment as a way to keep the people satisfied and prevent revolts.

The end result was not only the loss of human lives but many thousands of animals as well. Rome's wild animal hunts took an especially big toll on Africa's predators, like the "big cats" Ranger smells in the amphitheater's basement. Historians now believe that lions became extinct in Libya as a direct result of so many animals being captured and brought to Rome for these staged hunts.

Poets and writers were among the first to criticize the arena executions, wild animal hunts, and gladiator fights, hundreds of years before they ended. Historians have translated a letter that the poet Seneca wrote, urging his friends not to attend the games:

> *Unhappy as I am, how have I deserved that I must look on such a scene as this? Do not, my Lucilius, attend the games, I pray you. Either you will be corrupted by the multitude, or, if you show disgust, be hated by them. So stay away.*

While Seneca died in 64 AD, it would be hundreds of years before the gladiator games came to an end. The last known fight at the Colosseum happened in 404 AD. Through archaeology and the study of historical documents and works of art, historians are still working to understand this world of the gladiators.

In fact, ancient Rome itself is still being uncovered and discovered every day. On one of our Rome city tours, the guide pointed out a sign that referred to Subway Line C, a project that has been delayed so many times, it's become a favorite joke in Rome. "It will never be done," our guide said, "because you cannot dig in Rome without finding ruins. Then you stop and call in the archaeologists. And then you dig again and whoa! More ruins."

He laughed in frustration at his city's public transit system. But I couldn't help feeling a sense of wonder over all of the secrets that Rome still keeps. Every new find is like waving away a bit more of the fog that separates us from this ancient culture. With each discovery, we learn a little more and can have a clearer picture of what life might have been like for the people of ancient Rome.

GLOSSARY

amphitheater: An open-air venue used for entertainment and sporting events; the site of wild animal hunts, executions, and gladiator fights in ancient Rome.

baths: Public spaces where ancient Romans from all levels of society came to exercise, socialize, and wash themselves.

bestiarii: Men trained to hunt wild animals in the arena for entertainment in ancient Rome. They are also sometimes called *venatores*.

emperor: The ruler of ancient Rome.

familia gladiatoria: The Latin name for the "family of gladiators" in ancient Rome.

fire brigade: The ancient Roman fire department, responsible for bringing buckets of water and trying to isolate Rome's many fires to keep them from spreading.

Forum: The center of business and government in ancient Rome.

gladiator: A trained fighter, often a slave, who entertained the masses in ancient Rome.

Ludus Magnus: Rome's large gladiator school and training center, next to the Flavian Amphitheater (or Colosseum, as it's known today).

palus: A wooden stake that gladiators used for training.

pompa: The parade that marked the start of a day of gladiator games at a Roman amphitheater.

Porta Triumphalis: Latin phrase that means "Triumph Gate." This is how winning gladiators left the arena after a fight.

retiarius: A type of gladiator in ancient Rome who wore little armor but carried a net and trident.

secutor: A type of gladiator in ancient Rome who

wore a full metal helmet and carried a long shield and sword.

trident: A long spear with three prongs that resembles a pitchfork and was historically used for fishing.

FURTHER READING

To learn more about ancient Rome, gladiators, and working dogs, check out these books and websites:

Eyewitness Ancient Rome by Simon James (DK Publishing, 1990)

Sniffer Dogs: How Dogs (and Their Noses) Save the World by Nancy Castaldo (Houghton Mifflin Harcourt, 2014)

You Wouldn't Want to Be a Roman Gladiator!: Gory Things You'd Rather Not Know by John Malam (Franklin Watts, 2012)

"The Colosseum: Building the Arena of Death," from the BBC
http://www.bbc.co.uk/history/ancient/romans/launch_ani_colosseum.shtml

"The Colosseum: Emblem of Rome," also from the BBC

http://www.bbc.co.uk/history/ancient/romans/colosseum_01.shtml

"The Roman Empire," from PBS

http://www.pbs.org/empires/romans/

SOURCES

I'd like to offer my sincere thanks to Mark Posanza, a member of the Classics faculty at the University of Pittsburgh, who read this manuscript and offered guidance on everything from the naming of gladiators to the Latin plural for the fighters who took on wild animals. He was gracious with his time and a tremendous help.

I'd also like to thank the Walks of Italy guides who patiently answered my questions during tours of the Colosseum, Forum, Palatine Hill, and Pompeii. (I should also probably apologize to the innocent bystanders who had to endure all of those nitty-gritty details during our group tours.) The following resources were also incredibly helpful:

Adkins, Lesley, and Roy A. Adkins. *Handbook to Life in Ancient Rome*. New York: Oxford University Press, 1994.

Baker, Alan. *The Gladiator: The Secret History of Rome's Warrior Slaves*. New York: St. Martin's Press, 2001.

Balsdon, J. P. V. D. *Life and Leisure in Ancient Rome*. New York: McGraw-Hill, 1969.

Casson, Lionel. *Everyday Life in Ancient Rome*. Baltimore: Johns Hopkins University Press, 1998.

Coarelli, Filippo, and Ada Gabucci. *The Colosseum*. Los Angeles: J. Paul Getty Museum, 2001.

Cooley, Alison, and M. G. L. Cooley. *Pompeii: A Sourcebook*. London: Routledge, 2004.

Gabucci, Ada. *Rome*. Berkeley: University of California Press, 2007

Meijer, Fik. *The Gladiators: History's Most Deadly Sport*. Translated by Liz Waters. New York: St. Martin's Press, 2003

Plass, Paul. *The Game of Death in Ancient Rome: Arena Sport and Political Suicide*. Madison, WI: University of Wisconsin Press, 1995.

Rawson, Beryl. *Children and Childhood in Roman Italy*. Oxford: Oxford University Press, 2003.

Rawson, Beryl. *The Family in Ancient Rome: New Perspectives*. Ithaca, NY: Cornell University Press, 1986.

About the Author

Kate Messner is the author of *The Brilliant Fall of Gianna Z.*, recipient of the E. B. White Read Aloud Award for Older Readers; *Capture the Flag*, a Crystal Kite Award winner; *Over and Under the Snow*, a *New York Times* Notable Children's Book; and the Marty McGuire chapter book series. A former middle-school English teacher, Kate lives on Lake Champlain with her family and loves reading, walking in the woods, and traveling. Visit her online at www.katemessner.com.

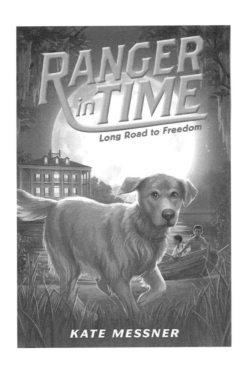

Ranger travels to a plantation in Maryland during the time of American slavery, where he meets a young girl named Sarah. When she learns that the plantation owner has plans to sell her little brother, she decides there's only one way to run — north.